Lee Aucoin, *Creative Director*
Jamey Acosta, *Senior Editor*
Heidi Fiedler, *Editor*
Produced and designed by
Denise Ryan & Associates
Illustration © Tracie Grimwood
Rachelle Cracchiolo, *Publisher*

Teacher Created Materials

5301 Oceanus Drive
Huntington Beach, CA 92649-1030
http://www.tcmpub.com
Paperback: ISBN: 978-1-4333-5489-2
Library Binding: ISBN: 978-1-4807-1145-7
© 2014 Teacher Created Materials

The Princess and the Pea

A Retelling of
Hans Christian Andersen's
Story

Written by Nicholas Wu
Illustrated by Tracie Grimwood

Once upon a time, there was a prince who wanted to marry a princess.

He met many princesses. But he was never sure they were *real* princesses.

The prince was very sad. He wanted to meet a real princess.

7

One night, during a fierce storm, there was a knock at the palace door.

The king found a girl standing in the rain.
Her clothes were wet. Water was dripping
from her hair. She needed a warm place
to sleep.

"Will you help a princess in need?" she asked.
"I promise I am a real princess."

"We'll soon find out," said the queen.
She went to the bedroom where the girl
would sleep.

She placed a single pea on the bed. Only a real princess would notice it.

Then, she piled twenty mattresses on top.

15

In the morning, the queen asked the girl, "Did you sleep well?"

"Sadly, I did not," said the girl. "I felt something hard in my bed."

The queen smiled. The princess had felt the pea through twenty mattresses. The prince had found a real princess!

In time, they were married. And they lived happily together.

This may or may not be a real tale.